T0195554

Sugar Daddy

NEAL LANDER

authorHOUSE

AuthorHouse™
1663 Liberty Drive
Bloomington, IN 47403
www.authorhouse.com
Phone: 1 (800) 839-8640

This is a work of fiction. All of the characters, names, incidents, organizations, and dialogue
in this novel are either the products of the author's imagination or are used fictitiously.

Published by AuthorHouse 02/19/2020

ISBN: 978-1-7283-4768-4 (sc)
ISBN: 978-1-7283-4767-7 (e)

Print information available on the last page.

Any people depicted in stock imagery provided by Getty Images are models,
and such images are being used for illustrative purposes only.
Certain stock imagery © Getty Images.

This book is printed on acid-free paper.

Every work of fiction is a collaboration of sorts because we utilize our experiences as well as our interactions and imagination to create an imaginary situation. That being said I must say thank you to everyone in and out of my life. Special thanks to God and my family. Thank you Star for getting this thing rolling. You were the jump off and I am forever grateful. Thank you to Shannon for being my female go to editor in chief. Your help was very instrumental in making this project possible.

Sugar Daddy

Welcome to Versions of life. These are a series of short stories designed to give the reader a glimpse into the mind and life of strangers. The events are real even if the names and specifics aren't all together factual. We are all living our own version of life unique to us. Sometimes we can relate to another person's version. Perhaps your version and someone else's version have similar elements. Similarities not withstanding each version of life is unique and cannot be copied. Sugar daddy is the first installment of this series and the next version shall be coming shortly. Be on the lookout for it my friends. Open your minds and enjoy this opportunity to witness a version of life.

Idlewild, Michigan 1979. The sky was crystal clear like blue topaz and a slight breeze was welcomed on this sticky July morning. The actual temperature was 78 degrees at 10am. The sun hadn't begun it's attack yet, but you could feel it coming. "This day is too pretty for a funeral" The little boy thought to himself. He was sad about the funeral but his young mind didn't fully comprehend the finality of death. He just wanted his dad to wake up and wrestle with him or tickle him like he used to do. But there was no coming back for this child's father. The

1

man had passed unexpectedly from a heart attack. He seemed so healthy everyone would say. The man left behind an only son and his wife.

Life crept on sadly for the little boy. He missed his dad very much. "Why did my dad leave us?" the kid postulated. It's hard on anyone to lose a loved one, and it was very hard on this youngster. His mom was hurt also. She cried herself to sleep many nights. She cried to her only son too. "What will we do baby?" she asked him redundantly. He silently wondered what would they do. Me and mom against the world he thought. School felt different. His friends, his teachers, even people he didn't know treated him differently. So many people knew his dad and they pitied the little boy whom had just lost his dad.

A year and a few months later his mom met a man. The man seemed nice enough thought the little boy. He seemed to take a sincere interest in the little boy. They played catch together, went to movies, swimming, and various activities together. A little over a year after that his mom married the nice man and the little boy's life changed again. Growing up in Idlewild, Michigan was pretty laid back. They lived on a dirt road with no street lights surrounded by wilderness. The little boy's step dad would take him camping from time to time. They spent quite a bit of time alone and it all seemed normal from the outside. After all the man didn't have any kids previously and the boy had lost his dad. That's what made it so shocking when allegations of sexual abuse arose. It was alleged that the man had been having sex with the little boy. The charges couldn't be proven and were subsequently dropped. After that the family left Michigan for a life somewhere else. Away from the scandal mongers the man called them.

Present day; I miss being a little girl. I miss having no responsibilities. Most of all I miss being innocent. There was a time when I thought I knew it all. There was a time when I thought that I was the shit. No man could resist my charms I would brag to my friends. Sure, there were plenty of pretty girls with big butts or big tits, but my butt was just right and so were my breasts. My cocoa complexion was on point as well. I used to be so hot in the ass. That's what the old heads called it. I can't explain the way I felt with a simple expression like hot in the ass. It was much more than that. I was curious and excited about sex. My friends and I were consumed by it, and we all experimented with boys our age or maybe a little older. The boys didn't do it for me. Even the real cute popular boys couldn't hold my interest. I gravitated to the older guys, but never hooked up with one until I turned 17. I wish that I never would have crossed that line because there is no going back now. Isn't it funny how a person can look back on past thoughts and behaviors and wonder how you ever thought and acted that way? Sometimes it's all good because we grow from our mistakes. Sometimes it's all bad because our mistakes can cause harm to our loved ones, or we never get a chance to grow because we die from our mistakes. I didn't die from my mistakes, but I'm heartbroken and in deep regret over my actions.

My name is Monay Haskins and I was 17 years old when I started down the dark road that brought this story to life. My little brother Jason Jr and I were raised by my father big Jason. When I was five years old my mom passed away. Jason Jr was four months old at the time she left us. All we ever knew was my dad, and he was always there for us through it all. We lived in Dayton, Ohio, a relatively small city located about 45 minutes from Cincinnati. I admired my dad because he was always so strong. He smiled through all the pain I know he had to feel. He was 30 years old when my mom passed, but he never remarried. I never even met another woman although I know he has had a few girlfriends. He would never bring them around us. One night I woke up around 2:30 am and was surprised to hear a woman's voice in the living room. I peeked in at them as they laughed and talked, and I could see that my dad was enjoying himself. I always wanted the best for my dad. I wished he could find his soul mate and be happy. Whenever I would mention him getting a girlfriend or a wife, he would give the same answer "I have you and little J and that's all I need". Everyone deserves happiness, right? Everyone deserves some type of joy out of this life, right? My poor dad was so sad even though he tried his best to hide it from us. We could see through the façade.

We grew up pretty normal, I guess. My brother and I have always been very close. People would say that my dad spoiled us rotten, but I don't agree. Overall dad was always laid back and easy going. There were only three things he demanded of us. Do our best in school, never

3

be a follower always think for ourselves, and keep our house clean. We had family vacations every year growing up. Just us three. The three amigos. I really miss those days. Those were happy times. My favorite vacation was a camping trip we had in the Colorado mountains. It was so beautiful up there above the clouds looking down on the city of Denver. The air was so crisp, and fresh. We drank water from a stream. Ice cold, clear, fresh water. We slept under the stars in our tent. I imagined a bear terrorizing us in the night but the only wild life we encountered were deer and rabbits. Reminiscing about those days always brings me a joy inside, but it also brings profound sadness and regret. Going back to those happy times is never an option save the memories that linger in my mind.

As we became older for some reason, I started to want another female's company. I really can't say why I felt that way, maybe me being the only girl all the time was getting to me. When I was 12 or 13, I started spending more time with my girl friends. We could relate to each other in ways my dad or my brother couldn't. The girls and I would talk about boys, sex, menstrual cycles, you know? All the stuff I couldn't really get into with my dad or my brother. My little brother didn't like the changes I was going through. How could he possibly understand? Him and my dad were guys and they couldn't understand the way another female could. As time flew by, we experimented with boys. Kissing and rubbing and dry humping were fun pastimes my friends and I would laugh about. Being bad girls was all the rage we thought. Nothing was undoable in our young hearts. We literally had the world by the balls as far as we were concerned. Being young, horny, and naïve amounts to a toxic mixture that leaves so many of us with our own set of regrets. As my life has taught me it's lessons, I have wasted time unwilling to learn. Only after dramatic and sometimes terrible consequences did stuff "click" for me.

When I turned 15, I felt omnipotent, I thought I was everything. My body was starting to develop into something nice if I do say so myself and guys were noticing me much more these days. My dad and I were always arguing over something or another. Little J got to be so nerve wracking now that we fought all the time too. Thank goodness

4

I had my girls to confide in. I had three friends that I considered close to me. Allison, Destiny, and Camryn were my road dogs, and I hung with them all the time. Allison was light skinned and pretty, and she developed a figure that made her age undeterminable if you didn't already know her. Older guys were hitting on Allison since we were in the 6th grade, and she would flirt and basically toy with them and tell us the hilarious stories. Destiny was the sweet heart of the group. She was a chocolate beauty, but she was always humble and down played how pretty she was. Camryn was the smart one I must say. She was always ahead of us as far as grades and school. Camryn was very pretty but she was a huge tomboy. She grew up the baby with four older brothers. The tension at home made me not want to be there, so I tried my best to stay away from home as much as possible. My friends were my escape from the mundane and often aggravating scene at home with my dad and JJ.

Time seemed to fly by at this time and the next week coming up was my sweet 16. My dad tried, I guess. He wanted me to talk to him, but I would just ask him to leave me alone. He went all out even though I was being a mean little bitch towards him. My birthday was awesome. My girls and I had a suite all to ourselves. We had snuck some wine and alcohol into our room, and we had invited some boys over. Everything was going great until Allison started making lude comments about my dad. "Girl your dad is hot", "I would bone your dad in a heartbeat", etc., etc. At first, I laughed it off because we were buzzing, but she just kept on with the comments. The other girls started joining in with her, and they all were laughing hysterically. I got mad and told them I would kick their ass if they kept it up. Finally, after a while I laughed along with them and started talking about their fathers or brothers. The boys never showed up and we laughed and joked until we all fell asleep on one bed.

As the following weeks went by, I tried to be nicer to my brother and my dad. My girls would sleep over my house some weekends, and Allison would flirt with my dad. She also flirted with JJ, but he wasn't into girls at that time. She was really starting to get on my nerves with her constant prancing and flirting. I didn't even want her at my house anymore, so I made it a point to ignore her calls and her presence at school. Here I am a junior in high school and this hot little bitch wants to fuck my dad. After a few days of me ignoring her she confronted me and asked what was going on. I told her that she wasn't welcome at my house anymore because of her constant flirtatious behavior towards my father. She looked at me and smiled and, said "That's why I'm fucking your dad bitch!". At first, I was caught off guard and speechless, but then I recovered and punched her as hard as I could. I just kept punching her in her foul mouth. A teacher pulled me off her and held me from hitting her more. Her mouth was swollen and bloody and she wept loudly "You bitch!" she cried. I felt a huge feeling of satisfaction sweep over me as I watched her being led away towards the nurse's office.

As I sat in the office waiting for my dad to come pick me up two police officers came in the office greeted by the school principal. I started getting nervous thinking this bitch going to press charges on me. Soon after the cops showed up my father walked in and straight away asked me what was going on. I was about to explain to him, but the cops came and placed my dad under arrest. I was stunned. I just sat there for several minutes until I was brought back to reality by the principal talking to me. "Are you ok dear?" she asked. All I could do was get up and walk away. Away from that office, away from that school, away from everything. It was like I could hardly breathe. I was crying hard and uncontrollably as I walked. I was so hurt feeling as if I had gotten my dad into trouble. Would he or could he ever forgive me for this? I already didn't have a mom, could I be about to lose my dad too? As I walked my mind raced over the events leading up to this. Did Camryn and Destiny know about this shit? If they both knew and never told me about it, I was going to kick their asses too. I wondered how long this had been going on and is it really true. So much to think about. What was going to happen to JJ and me if our dad goes to prison?

My dad was released that same evening and all charges were dropped. He came home looking beaten and defeated. JJ greeted him shouting "hey daddy, hey daddy, hey daddy" as he laughed happily. My dad smiled at him and said, "hey big man". He looked at me and said we need to talk. I just shook my head in agreement because we really did need to talk. He had some serious explaining to do, and I wanted some answers. He explained to me how he had made a mistake and slept with Allison one night several months ago. She had crept into his room while I was sleep and slid into his bed naked. "At first I thought I was dreaming" he said. "It all happened so fast, I'm so sorry baby girl. Please forgive me" he stammered. "How can I forgive you dad?" I asked. "Do you realize how embarrassing it will be when I go to school tomorrow?" I continued. All I could do was cry. "Why are you out of jail dad?" I asked. "Allison is under age and you're a grown ass man." I continued. "Well in Ohio the age of consent is 16" he mumbled. "Which means she is old enough to consent to us having sex legally" he continued. "Allison told the cops that the episode was consensual" he mumbled softly. "I will transfer you to any school you want baby girl" he stated. "I want out of this city dad" I yelled.

The next few days were a blur because my dad transferred me to a high school in Cincinnati. I have to give him credit he made that move happen fast. He put our house up for sale and even transferred JJ to a new school in our new city. We moved into an apartment for the time being. I was still very upset with my father though. All of this was totally unnecessary if only he could have kept his dick in his pants. How many times had they slept together I wondered? He made it seem like it was just the one time, but I wonder if he was leaving some things out. That bitch Allison made it seem like they were boning on the regular. Now we had to move, change schools, meet new people, make new friends. I knew I wasn't bringing anymore friends around my dad. He wasn't to be trusted at all. I wonder how he would feel if I messed around with one of his friends or an older man. A man around his age. He already let me know that it was legal. That's the answer, that's how I will get back at my dad for fucking my friend. I will get me a sugar daddy. I was suddenly in a much better mood. "Now how do I find me a sugar daddy?" I thought to myself.

I checked out a couple guys in our complex, but they weren't what I was looking for. I wanted a man in his early 40's just like my dad. He had to be single or separated, he had to have money. Nice place to stay, nice car, and he definitely had to be good looking. I told my dad that I wanted to get a job. I figured that I would try to get a job in a jewelry store. I'm an excellent saleswoman, and I would meet guys with money there. After all, how many broke guys buy jewelry? I thought I had it all figured out. After several applications submitted and a couple interviews, I gave up on the jewelry store gig. I started looking elsewhere and came upon a hardware store position. I got the job straightaway and I was enjoying it. This stuff was interesting. Home makeovers captured my imagination. I was learning all about different trades like plumbing, electric, HVAC, and several other building trades. Many creepy older guys would flirt with me some even offered me money for a date. None of them fit what I was looking for plus I didn't want no thirsty ass dude. I was very picky, but I knew exactly what I wanted. To my surprise I met a potential sugar daddy in just my 5th or 6th day on the job.

His name was Tyler and he was handsome, he drove a very nice pickup truck. I didn't know his age, but he had slight gray in his beard and hair. I noticed him a few times in the store. He was obviously a regular customer. He was always polite and nice when he came through my line, but totally uninterested in me at all. I tried giving him my best smile. I tried making small talk. Nothing was getting through to this guy. I had to be a bit more aggressive with him because he wasn't catching on to my subtle suggestions. This went on for several weeks until I saw my chance and went for it. I was on break when Tyler pulled up in the parking lot. I was sitting on a bench close to the entrance. "Hello Mr. Tyler" I cooed. "Hi Ms. Monay" he responded. "I'm good just starving a bit. Would you be kind enough to take me to grab a bite before my break is over?" I asked him. He paused for several seconds and then said, "sure why not your always nice to me when I come to the store". Tyler was kind of tall over six feet I would surmise, and he was light brown like milk chocolate. He looked strong too like he worked out regularly. My attraction was very strong for this stranger. I wondered if we would ever really hook up as we walked towards his vehicle.

After we got into his truck, I started to second guess this whole sugar daddy thing. I was nervous as heck, but then I thought about how Allison had seduced my dad and resolved to follow through. I asked him if he was married and he responded in the negative. We made small talk mostly because I was trying to feel him out. He was a total gentleman very polite. I was feeling at ease, so I just flat out asked him if he would ever consider a relationship with someone like me. He was clearly shaken by the question, and he was quiet for a moment. He looked me in the eyes and said, "no I have never thought about that and I would never consider it either." He continued "I'm old enough to be your father baby girl, and I'm not a pedophile dear". I was stunned by his response. "Am I ugly or something?" I thought because this isn't how it's supposed to be going. He must have read my mind because he said "You're a beautiful young lady and if I was 25 years younger, I would shoot my shot. You will meet a young man in your age group baby girl just be patient". "What would your father think about you having a relationship with my old ass?" he asked redundantly. I didn't even respond. He drove me back to the store and left.

I was very disappointed by this turn of events, but I did respect his honesty and respect for my virtue if that's what it was. Either way I wanted him even more now. I wasn't a virgin nor was I experienced at sex and seduction. I need a professional opinion and advice on how to snag this reluctant big fish. The only person I knew that had this type of experience was Allison, but we had fallen out and I didn't want her all in my business anyway. I needed her expertise though so I had to figure out how I was going to go about bleeding her for info. I sent a text to Allison apologizing for the altercation and explaining how I had felt at the time. I didn't know what to expect from her, if she would even respond or anything. I also reached out to Destiny and Camryn to see what the buzz was around school and our old neighborhood. Destiny called me back right away "Hey girl, how are you? I miss you so much". I told her that I was fine and that I miss her too. I explained why I had changed my number and deleted all my social media accounts. I just wanted to disappear at that time. She was very understanding, and I was reminded how much of a sweetheart Destiny was over the years. I asked her if she had any prior knowledge of Allison's behavior. She adamantly denied any knowledge of it and told me that she hadn't even talked to her any more since the scandal came out. We talked for over an hour just kind of getting reacquainted with each other.

Camryn hit me up the next day, and we pretty much went over the same things Destiny and I had discussed. The only difference being that Camryn said she had suspicions of Allison before everything came out, but she wasn't positive about it and didn't want to start something over nothing. Turns out her suspicions were valid, but it's too late to do anything now. She still apologized for not alerting me ahead of time, but I stopped her and let her know that I understood her position. That kind of thing is hard to bring up specially if you're not positive about it. I didn't discuss my sugar daddy plans with either of my friends. I didn't want them talking any sense to me. My mind was made up now and I was going to fuck that man really, really, good. While we were talking, I received a text from Allison. She was apologetic and regretful about the entire situation. She accepted the blame for it and hoped I could forgive her. I told Camryn that I would call her back later and got off the phone, so I could text Allison back.

Allison and I exchanged text messages back and forth a few times before I called her. I was tired of texting, and I had questions to ask her without evidence of a text. We started out with small talk catching up and at the same time feeling each other out. I apologized for losing my cool and punching her, and she apologized for sleeping with my dad. I was glad to get that mess over with because I wanted to pick her brain about snagging an older guy. I casually asked, "have you been with any older guys besides my dad?". There was a long pause and I wondered if I had moved too soon on speaking about this. Then she stammered, "why do you ask that? Has Destiny said something to you?". No no it's nothing like that. I told her how I was interested in an older guy and wanted to know how she pulled them. She was still hesitant I could sense it, so I tried to ease her mind by inviting her to lunch this weekend. She said ok and we decided to leave the conversation where it was at until we saw each other.

We met up at the mall early Saturday afternoon. The first thing out of Allison's mouth were questions about why I said what I said and why I asked what I asked. Why was I asking about older guys? Was I after her dad for revenge? I tried my best to calm her down and not bust my gut laughing at her discomfort. Here this bitch is going around fucking on people's fathers, but at the same time worrying about someone fucking hers. I assured her that I wasn't after her dad or anyone in her family. We grabbed some iced lattes and sat down to talk. I had tried unsuccessfully to control my laughter, because when we sat down I hollered like a hyena. She stared at me straight faced like what's funny bitch? I explained why in between fits of giggles, and slowly she joined me in laughing. She told me that she already felt really bad about the situation and didn't want me doing anything stupid because of what she did. I felt a small twinge of remorse, or second thoughts, I'm not sure what you would call that moment of clarity we all get before doing something stupid that we learn to regret too late. After the mistake we all remember that moment like "I wish I would have followed my first mind". I ignored my first mind and continued plotting on Mr. Tyler.

Allison explained like the obvious professional that she was, and I had my sponge out soaking it all in. She told me that the good older guys the ones that weren't perverted slime bags were extremely hard to get. "You have to be very patient and take everything slow" she said. These guys have careers, families, lots of shit to lose and they aren't going to risk it just to fuck a young bitch. I wondered why my dad risked his life for this young hot bitch, but that thought flashed across my mind and went away just as fast as it came. She must have read my mind because on cue she stated, "Your dad was the toughest that I have faced, and I have faced a few." I just waved my hand dismissively like whatever just continue the lesson teacher. She told me how to strategize alone time with the victim. The more time you can spend with him just the two of you the better. Always smell good, always have on sexy matching panties and bras, always have your nails and feet done, always be looking your best but never slutty. You must make sure he understands that you are young, but you got your mind right. Maturity is a must. Don't be all up in your phone when yall are together. Pay close attention to his likes and dislikes. Girl that shit is a winner for sure. They love for a bitch to listen and pay attention to them. And if all else fails try to catch him tipsy or get him tipsy and take the dick. She chuckled after that and looked me in the eyes and slowly said, "The golden rule of this shit is to keep your fucking mouth closed". "You see what happened when I opened my big mouth" she stated solemnly.

I thought about everything we had discussed and felt confident that I could play by the rules. Allison really was a pro; she could start her own school or classes on seduction. I couldn't wait to try some new moves on Tyler. I wondered if it would work on him. Allison interrupted my train of thought with more questions. Are you sure this is something you want to do? Why are you into older guys all of a sudden? I asked her why was she into older guys and she replied rather simply "young guys don't do anything for me at all. They're immature, self-absorbed, and they can't fuck like an older man does." I was taken aback by her candor, but I laughed and said, "damn tramp!" She laughed too and we both giggled for a few moments before she got serious again. "I'm not trying to preach or knock your game Monay, but at the same time I hope you're not doing this to get back at your dad for what happened between him and me. I paused for a second thinking about what she was asking me. "Girl I feel like you do. These young dudes can't fuck, they childish as hell, and they ain't got no damn money.", I replied. We both giggled for a moment and then Allison got serious again. "I really am sorry about what happened between your dad and me Monay. It wasn't your dad's fault for real.", she said. "Girl I understand my dad is kind of fine to be an old guy", I replied. She smiled and shook her head and we enjoyed the rest of our time together getting re-acquainted.

My dad had found us a nice very comfortable house in an area called Sharonville. It was a suburb of Cincinnati. Cincinnati is huge compared to little ass Dayton. I enjoyed the change of scenery even though I still bitched to my dad about having to move and all. Cincinnati was actually pretty nice. Maybe it was because it was all new to me. I had yet to make friends with anyone. I was actually afraid to make any new acquaintances because I didn't trust my dad around young girls my age. Was that why my dad never remarried or had a girlfriend? My thoughts were all over the place when it came to how I felt about my dad now. He had never shown any signs of being a fucking pervert before Allison. Then I had to honestly analyze the scenario. Allison was built like a brick shit house no lie. Allison had also been overly flirtatious with my dad constantly. None of that bullshit is an excuse for my dad, but I could understand him succumbing to the charms of Allison's fine ass. Hell, if I was into girls, I would fuck her in a heartbeat.

I was anxious to get back to work and bump into Tyler. I wanted to try out the stuff Allison had told me about on Mr. Tyler. A stroke of luck came my way when our hot water tank was on the fritz suddenly. My dad asked me if my job offered this service. I told him no but that I knew someone who could fix it or replace it. It was several days until he came back in the store. I was bubbling when he came in my line, but I was trying to play it cool. "Hello Mr. Tyler", I said coyly. He smiled and said hello back to me and asked how I was doing. I told him I was doing well but was wondering if he could come by my house and check out our hot water tank. He asked what the problem was, and I just told him that it wasn't working properly. I gave him my address and home number and told him my dad's name. He said he would give my dad a call and set something up, so I thanked him and bid him a great rest of his day. My plan was officially in motion now, and I was excited and nervous at the same time. I hope this man will learn to appreciate all the trouble I'm going through just to give him this young pussy. I laughed at the thought and enjoyed the rest of my shift. I'm sure that most people would say that I'm a hoe or a hot in the ass young bitch. Perhaps it's true. I really didn't care about anyone else's opinion then, and I couldn't care less now.

As the next several days went by, I was getting annoyed and impatient with this whole process. I was about ready to say the hell with Mr. Tyler when I received a call from my dad saying that he had an appointment on the day Tyler was coming to replace our water tank. He wanted to see if I could be there to let him in and watch over everything. Of course, I was wanting this scenario all along, so I agreed with no hesitation. When the day arrived, I was fresh, and clean, smelling good, looking good, groomed, manicured and pedicured. I wanted him to see me at my best, and I was leaving nothing to chance. This man was going to be mine he just didn't know it yet. I wore a pink shorts outfit that fit me good but wasn't tight either. I know that I was looking good and he would have to be a damn fool not to want this here. Tyler arrived but he wasn't alone. He had some ugly frog faced guy with him. "This is Tyrone Monay, Tyrone this is Ms. Monay" he introduced us smiling cheerfully. I promise I wanted to slap the shit out of him. I was pissed that he brought a fucking blocker with him. "Tyrone is going to be helping me Monay, this is heavy work for one person", he chimed. I just smiled and walked to my room. Fuck him I thought to myself. I'm done trying with this fool. I can find me another fine older man.

I steamed for about 40-45 minutes, but I eventually calmed myself and decided to be hospitable. I left my room to go check and see if they needed anything, a refreshment or whatever. Tyler was alone working with his back to me. He had on a t-shirt and I could see his muscles moving under that shirt. My pussy was starting to moisten when he turned around and caught me admiring him with pure lust in my eyes. "You want something to drink?" I stammered. He just smiled at me and shook his head yes. "What would you like?" I asked. "Water please, Ice cold water" he replied. As I turned to go get his water he startled me by grabbing my hand softly. "Does Tyrone want something too?" I asked. He didn't speak he just pulled me into his arms and kissed me tenderly. I melted into him like soft, warm caramel. I was totally stunned by this turn of events. He turned me around so that my back side was pressed into his hard manhood. Oh my God it feels so huge I was thinking to myself as he pulled my shorts and panties down to my ankles. "Tyrone has left baby. It's just me and you" he whispered huskily in my ear. "Is this what you want baby?" he asked as he entered me from behind. "Oh yes daddy" I gasped over and over. At that point I was awaken by a loud knock on my door. I was fucking dreaming. Geez! It felt so realistic. Oh, shit my panties were soaked like I had peed on myself. Then the knock on my door again. "WHAT IS IT!" I yelled angrily. "It's me, Tyler, Monay, we are finished with the water tank and about to leave" he said. "Oh, ok thank you. Have a good rest of your day" I yelled through the door. "You too bye bye" he said.

This was so crazy I had never in my life had a dream like that. It was so intense and real. I could actually feel him entering me. I had to go and take a hot bubble bath and wash away these thoughts and feelings I'm having for a man that don't even want my young dumb ass. I was seriously feeling young, dumb, and full of cum just like my panties were. Well enough of that bullshit for real. I'm getting me someone who want this good pussy I thought to myself. The next few days at work were uneventful and boring. I had absolutely zero prospects on the horizon, and my fucking coochie was yearning for some attention. I began to contemplate boning my ex-boyfriend up in Dayton, but that would be extremely difficult. For one thing that boy gets on my every nerve ending and jumps up and down. Another reason that would be so hard is because the boy just cannot fuck right. I'm not trying to make myself out to be a professional sex artist, but a person can feel when the shit is right or conversely when it's wrong. That whack ass sex with him was wrong.

My inane mumblings and thoughts were interrupted by Tyler waving at me. I waved back, and he proceeded to approach me. "How are you doing today pretty lady? He asked me casually. Hold the presses. Did he just say, "pretty lady?" to me? Maybe I'm tripping. I just replied dumbly "Hi". "So, are you mad at me or something?" he asked. "Umm no why would you think that?" I replied. "Well the way you were acting when we came to put in your new water tank. You went in your room and stayed the whole time we were there. You didn't even come out to say bye." he stated. I was still kind of shocked at this conversation we were having, but I still tried to play it cool. "I was just tired. I went in my room and fell asleep." I replied casually. "Oh, ok that's cool. I was just wondering. I have been thinking about what you had asked me in my truck. Maybe when you get time we can discuss things further." he mumbled nervously. I told him sure thing and wrote my cell phone number down on his receipt. "Call me and we will set something up" I stated cheerfully. He nodded and proceeded to leave the store with his purchases.

For the rest of the day I was on cloud nine floating through my duties happily. I could not believe the way things had turned out. I thought back to everything that had occurred over the past several days that led up to this. I wanted to pin point the moment I had broken through his armor. I wanted to know how I could repeat it if need be. Was it the outfit? I was looking cute if I do say so myself. Was it my attitude? "What was it?" I wondered. I couldn't figure out the exact moment or thing I did or didn't do that changed his mind. Well I can always ask him when we talk. I was anxious to have a conversation with him soon. Now I was confident that once I got him all to myself, I could seduce him completely. Tyler was about to be mine all mine. I thought back to that freaky dream I had about him and started to moisten all over again. This man turned me on that was for sure. I wondered if I was going to be able to turn him on the same way. Well I was going to find out for certain real soon and I could hardly wait. Tyler didn't call me until Friday evening. He wanted to meet me Saturday afternoon for lunch and conversation. I agreed, and we set up a quiet, low key location. I made sure I was smoking hot in a mini skirt and semi tight shirt. Lavender everything, skirt, shirt, nails, and toes too.

We met at an Italian joint on the outskirts of Cincinnati. I caught an Uber to the place because Tyler was going to drive me home after our date. I have always loved authentic Italian food. I was very excited about going all the way with Tyler. He must have been reading my mind because he got straight to the point. "Look Monay I really don't want you mad at me or hating me, but I cannot be with you the way you want me to" he stated. I instantly got pissed and asked him why we were even there. He tried reasoning with me saying that he wanted to be my friend. I was thinking to myself that this motherfucker must be retarded. I coldly looked him in the eyes and threatened him straight out. "You are going to take me to a nice hotel room after dinner Tyler. You are going to fuck me good Tyler. And if you don't, I will tell everyone that you are fucking me" I stated coldly. He was speechless for several minutes. Finally, he said "This is really what you want huh? You going to make me fuck you?" he continued. I shook my head yes. Then almost sadly like he was about to start crying he said ok.

The lunch was quiet as we ate our food. Tyler looked so damn sad and pitiful I almost felt sorry for him. I began to try to reassure him and put his mind at ease. "Tyler everything we do will always be our secret. I swear on my dead mama" I said solemnly. "I really like you and I want you to like me the same way" I continued. He started to at least get his color back as I spoke to him. "I'm not trying to brag but you are going to love this young pussy. A woman your age can't do it like I can daddy" I stated as seductively as I could. He smiled slightly at that comment and I gained confidence to continue. "Can we please just put aside our ages, the circumstances, and any negativity?" I asked him. "I want to give you my all Tyler and I want your all. Nothing else matters today daddy just you and me making sweet love" I continued. When we walked to his truck, I could tell that he was still nervous, but he was definitely better than before. Hell, you would have thought this motherfucker was on death row the way he was looking before I set his mind at ease. He opened my door for me and I reached over to open his for him. I held his hand all the way to the hotel.

The room was nice, and I was tingling with excitement. Tyler was still quiet and acting all sad and shit like he didn't really want this young pussy. I almost felt sorry for him and let him off the hook, but I quickly changed my mind when I remembered the dream I had. I approached him and embraced him tenderly. "Don't act like this Tyler. Please make love to me." I whispered softly. I kissed him on the mouth and after a few moments he started kissing me back. We began undressing each other recklessly almost ripping our clothes off. When we were both naked, we stood there staring at each other in the eyes for several anxious moments. Then he lifted me off my feet and placed me on the bed. He opened my legs and put his head between my thighs and began to lick me and kiss me and suck my pussy softly and slowly. Oh my goodness that shit felt so good I was trembling with pleasure as my pussy creamed in his mouth. I screamed inadvertently. I had never felt like this. How could anything feel this damn good? Was this shit normal? I began to squirm and push his head away, but he kept on doing it. He was stronger than me and I couldn't make him stop. I was loudly whimpering in ecstasy. After I couldn't even try to struggle against him anymore he got on top of me and entered me slowly and forcefully. I was in nirvana now. This man knew how to fuck. I came and came and kept coming until he came and lay next to me glistening lightly with sweat. I was asleep in seconds.

I woke up some time later looking for the clock because I wanted to get home before my dad started worrying about where I was. It was only 8:45 in the evening so I relaxed. It felt like I had been asleep longer than that. I glanced over at Tyler and he was awake staring at me. I was startled to see him looking at me like that. "Do you regret this Tyler?" I asked. He remained silent staring at me blankly. "This was the greatest sex I have ever had Tyler. Please don't be upset with me" I continued breathlessly. I continue talking to him explaining to him how I felt and about the dream I had about him. He finally spoke, "I don't regret it at all baby. I love you. We will always be together" he said flatly. I studied his face to see if he was playing around with me. I think this fucker is serious I thought. Fuck it I thought, if he keeps giving me that put your ass to sleep dick, he can say whatever he wanted to. I made him fuck me again before taking me home. I felt so damn good walking in the house. It was a little before 10 and my little brother greeted me. "Where you been Monay?" he asked. I ignored his question and hugged him and kissed his forehead. He wiped off my kiss in disgust. I laughed and went to my room floating.

The next day was great also. Good sex will have a girl feeling high on life for real because there was nothing bothering me on this day. I was happy and cheerful to everyone all day at school. Even the little bitches that I didn't like received waves and smiles. I texted Tyler good morning and have a great day. He sent me the same with hearts and kisses attached. I hoped he would come to my job today because I wanted to look at him. I really wanted to do more than that, but I didn't want him getting tired of me too fast. Work was going just as lovely as school went and everything was peachy. Tyler finally made an appearance halfway through my shift. He was smiling at me warmly and I honestly started getting moist at the thought of what he did to me yesterday. This man was the shit. I thanked my lucky stars for finding him. He came through my line smiling. "I have a surprise for you Monay" he said. My co-worker looked at him and then at me shaking her head and mumbling under her breath. Fuck that bitch I thought. "What you got for me big daddy?" I whispered. He asked me what time I got off work and said he would show me then. I was excited and curious about my surprise. Come on seven o'clock I thought.

I got off work practically running out that building to see what

Tyler was surprising me with. He was standing in the parking lot next to a convertible sports car with his arms folded smiling from ear to ear. I was like wow he bought a new car a real nice car too. "You can't do home improvements in that car Tyler" I joked and laughed. "Ha ha" he said sarcastically. "This is your car baby" he continued. I was shocked into silence standing there looking stupid with my mouth open for several seconds. I never would have guessed he was surprising me with a new car. Oh my goodness. How was I gonna explain this to my dad? He must have been reading my mind because he stated that I could park it at his place. "Soon it will be your place too baby" he stated seriously. "Let's go for a spin" I shouted happily. I look back at that moment now and cannot for the life of me understand why that didn't scare me. I just knew I had everything under control. Little did I know what I had gotten myself and my family into. Hind sight is 20/20.

As the next few weeks went by, I was happy as I had ever been. Tyler gave me whatever I asked for and a bunch of stuff I didn't ask for but was glad that he got them for me. Clothes, jewelry, money, it was a dream come true. And the sex continued to be absolutely mesmerizing. He was the best I had obviously made a great choice when I picked him to be mine. As we were eating dinner one evening Tyler asked me if I would be willing to spend the rest of my life with him. I looked him in the eye and responded "I will be with you forever Tyler. I love you". I truly meant what I said to him at that moment. But the fact was that I was seventeen years young and couldn't fathom what I was really saying. At the time everything felt so right, I couldn't ask for more. Allison was talking shit saying that I had outdone her in the sugar daddy department. I was like shit he ain't my sugar daddy girl he my fucking husband to be. We would laugh and celebrate like we had not a care in the world. Tyler had asked me to move in with him, but I told him I had to graduate first. My dad was suspicious about where I was getting all my fancy clothes and jewelry from, but he was quiet about it. My graduation was a little over a month away I was ready for school to be over with. I was ready to move in with my king and be his princess.

About a week later Allison and I were out shopping and enjoying our day at the mall when we were approached by two guys around our age. We laughed at them and told them to beat it. They continued to follow us and make lewd comments about our anatomy among other things. I wasn't bothered at all. Out of nowhere Tyler walks up to them and tells them to get lost or get hurt. "My bad grandpa" one of them blurted out smartly. Tyler grabbed him and punched him several times until he slumped to the floor bloody. He turned to the other guy, but he took off running. It all happened so fast I couldn't react fast enough. "Tyler what is wrong with you?" I asked. The mall security approached us quickly and Tyler explained that the young man on the floor had been harassing Allison and I. He told them he had intervened, and the young man had attacked him, so he had to defend himself. Allison looked at me and I looked at her but we both remained silent and allowed Tyler to tell the story. We both agreed somewhat hesitantly to everything he said. The mall cops took our statements and told us we were free to leave. On the way home Allison and I tried to make heads or tails of what had just occurred. "Your man is crazy girl" she blurted out. I just shook my head in agreement.

Later that evening at Tyler's house I finally had an opportunity to ask him about earlier. He looked at me straight away and said calmly that he would kill anyone who bothered me. I was taken aback by the finality of his statement. He was very serious. This was the first time I remember being truly frightened in his presence. He also told me that we were getting married after I graduated. Before that day I was glad to discuss the future with Tyler, but now I was having second thoughts. I didn't want to piss him off any more so of course I agreed with whatever he said. Have any of you out there ever had an epiphany about someone that you had known for some time? Thought you knew them and then BAM! You finally see all the things you had been missing. That's the way I felt at that moment about Tyler. This son of a bitch was crazy as hell. I made up my mind right then and there that I was going to get the hell away from him before he snapped again. When I left his house that day, I had no intentions of ever going back there again. I intended to avoid his fruity ass forever.

The next day at work I received flowers from Tyler. I was ignoring his calls and texts. Right before it was time for me to get off work, he showed up at my register smiling. "Hi there beautiful" he said softly. I looked at him without responding. "What's wrong baby?" he asked. "We need to take a break for a while Tyler" I stated calmly. "I will be returning the car and the gifts back to you later on today" I continued. He looked at me like I was talking in a foreign language. Then he shook his head no and said that everything he gave me was mine regardless if we were together or not. Allison walked up at that moment smiling. "Hi yawl" she stated cheerfully. Tyler turned at the sound of her voice and stared at her coldly. Then he just walked away. "What's his deal?" she asked. I grabbed her hand and proceeded to go to the time clock, so I could clock out for the day. I explained what had occurred right before she had walked up. I told her that I was scared of Tyler. She laughed at my fears. "Girl you done fucked that man really good" she blurted out. "He ain't going nowhere" she continued. "How do I get rid of his weird ass?" I asked. "He will get the hint soon as you quit answering his text and calls" she stated. I thought about that and hoped she was right. She had been right about so many other things that had led up to this situation.

JJ woke me early the next morning with the sad news that Allison had been run over by a car. "Huh??" I stuttered still half sleep. "She's in critical condition in ICU right now" he stated sadly. He had tears in his eyes, so I hugged him as I started to sob on his shoulder. After I had cried and calmed myself down, I got cleaned up and dressed and headed out to the hospital to check on my friend. I was sad about this turn of events not just because Allison was my friend. I also didn't have anyone else I could talk to and confide in about my Tyler situation. The news was that she had been hit by a dark colored SUV. The driver never stopped so the police were looking for any help catching the hit and run criminal. She was out of surgery and stable when I arrived at the hospital. These damn Dayton drivers cannot fucking drive I thought to myself. Allison's family were all in the waiting area as I walked up her mom hugged me tightly. "The doctor said she's going to be ok praise God" she said tearfully. "How are you doing mommy?" I asked her through teary eyes. She explained to me all that she knew so far. She said the driver had drove up on the sidewalk to hit her. The police were thinking either the driver was impaired or that they had purposely hit Allison.

A shiver traveled up my spine as I thought about someone hitting her on purpose. Would Tyler do that? My mind was racing. No, he couldn't possibly be that damn crazy I reasoned to myself. The idea was definitely on my mind when my thoughts were interrupted by questions from her family members. "Was she beefing with anyone?" they asked. "No not that I know of" I responded glumly. "I can't imagine someone doing such a thing" I continued. "You and Allison were just fighting not that long ago" yelled her brother. "So what?" I replied. "We have been made up and have been hanging out almost daily ever since then" I continued. An awkward silence followed our exchange. I would have left if I wasn't concerned about my girl. Destiny and Camryn made an appearance at that moment and I was glad to see them. After they both greeted the family, we all hugged and began to chat amongst ourselves for a little while. Every one of us was saddened and shocked about Allison. We all waited patiently for some good news about Allison's condition. The doctor finally appeared and assured us that she was going to be fine, but they had her sedated, so we should all get some rest. He told us she would be ready to receive visitors in a day or two. Everyone but her mom and dad left shortly thereafter with them assuring us that we would be contacted if anything changed.

As I drove back to Cincinnati my mind kept returning to Tyler. Would he?? Could he?? I was determined to find out, but also cautious. If he did do such a thing what else was he capable of? Allison could have been killed for Christ sake. The more I thought about it the more I began to believe that he did in fact try to kill Allison. But why? Why hurt her? It didn't make any sense. Maybe I was tripping because he had been acting so weird lately. Perhaps he didn't have anything at all to do with Allison's accident. Maybe one of her old guys was upset at her, or their children. After all I had tried to punch her lights out myself. I hated feeling like this. I was concerned about my friend, but I still had to try and analyze this incident objectively. The fact that Allison had been boning many older gentlemen made it difficult to try and figure who could be mad enough to try and kill her. I couldn't speak to her family or anyone for that matter because this older dude thing was between me and her. I was starting to regret ever beginning this thing with Tyler. I feared what he might be capable of. I was also paranoid about every car that passed by. Was I next?

I arrived home to an empty house, so I went into my room to lay down for a bit. I must have dozed off because I was awakened by a persistent door bell. I glanced at the time and realized that I had only napped for about 15 minutes. "Who is it" I yelled at the door as I approached it. "It's Tyler Monay" I heard from the other side of the door. Wow he had never come to my home before. I opened the door and stepped out onto the porch. "What's up Tyler?" I said quickly. "I miss you baby. Whatever I did I'm sorry. Please don't be avoiding me like this Monay." he replied glumly. "I have been busy Tyler" I replied. "My best friend was struck by a car and almost died" I continued. "She's ok?" he asked quickly. "Yes, she's going to be fine but the whole ordeal has worn me out" I said sadly. My dad's car pulled up at that moment and I was suddenly nervous about my dad seeing Tyler and me. Tyler stood there quietly looking at me. Little J ran up before my dad "Hi Monay" he shouted gladly. Before I could reply he continued into the house. My dad approached us smiling. "Hello there Mr. Tyler. Hey Monay" he said. "What are you two up to?" he continued. "How are you Jason" Tyler replied. "I was just leaving" he continued. Then he walked away.

"Damn what's eating him?" my dad asked to no one in particular. "And what's going on with you and him?" he continued looking me straight in the eye. "Tyler's my boyfriend dad" I replied. Before I realized what happened I was on my back. My dad had slapped me. Hard. I was dizzy for several seconds sitting on the ground holding my face where he had hit me. I couldn't believe it. My dad had never hit me before. He was furious. His entire face was beet red. He finally spoke again. "What the fuck do you call yourself doing Monay?" he asked slowly. I was still sitting on the porch speechless head ringing from the blow. "I hope you know what you're doing girl" he continued sadly. Then he turned and walked back to his car and left. As I sat there in pain and shock I started to cry. I wept for 10 or 15 minutes before JJ came outside. "What's wrong Monay?" he cried alarmingly. "Daddy slapped me" I whimpered. JJ just hugged me for several moments and then he whispered, "Why did dad hit you?" I explained the situation in between sobs. "Wow Monay. Dad's never hit us before." he stated flatly. "You must have hurt dad's feelings very bad" JJ continued. His words rang in my ears and I realized that he was correct in his assertion.

The next day I received word that Allison wanted to see me, so I drove to Dayton to visit her. During the drive my mind rehashed the events of the last few days. So much was happening so quickly. I needed a break from all of this. I had created this monster, so it was up to me to kill it. When I arrived at the hospital only Allison's mom remained. I hugged her and asked how things were going. "Allison has been asking for you since she woke up baby" her mom said. "I'm just glad my baby girl is going to be ok" she continued. I agreed with her and then turned to sit next to Allison's bed. Her mom left us alone to go get some coffee or something. Allison was asleep until I grabbed her hand. She looked at me for a moment before starting to speak. "Monay I am so sorry for what I did to your dad" she stated sadly. "Girl we are good" I started. She silenced me and blinked back tears from her eyes. "I black mailed your father into fucking me Monay" she whispered. "He would have never done it otherwise" she continued. I just sat there silently listening to her confession thinking about how similar my own situation was to hers. "I told your dad that if he didn't fuck me I was going to tell everyone that he had been fucking me anyway" she said slowly. Her words stung me to my core. I had blamed my dad. I had been so mad at my dad.

Allison told me that her near death experience had made her into a changed person. I stayed with her for several hours listening to her revelations and confessions. It was truly sad and at the same time illuminating. Her words made me look at my own train of thought and made me want to change my ways as well. Allison had no clue who tried to kill her. She assumed that it was someone who's dad she had been fucking. She couldn't think of any other reason someone would want her dead. While driving back home I thought about how I had manipulated Tyler. I was sad and sorry for how I had treated him. That man was living his life not bothering nobody until my hot ass came along. I resolved to release him and apologize for my behavior. He was a good man and deserved so much better than to be black mailed into a fake ass relationship with a teenager. As I drove, I realized that Tyler had fallen in love with me. At least that's what he said, but I believed him. He had spent several thousand dollars on me. He said he wanted to spend the rest of his life with me. This thing has gotten out of my control I thought. I owed Tyler a huge apology. I owed my father the same. Would either man be able to forgive me? I resolved to woman up and accept the consequences of my actions.

When I arrived back home my dad was sitting in the kitchen quietly brooding. I approached him and apologized to him about everything. I explained how I was upset with him, so I started the relationship with Tyler. My dad listened intently and hugged me tightly when I finished. "Baby you and JJ are all I live for" he stated. "Every day I pray for God to watch over and protect you both. I couldn't take it if something happened to you or little J" he continued. Tears were in my dad's eyes as he spoke to me. I felt like a huge piece of shit. I explained to him my plan to apologize and break it off with Tyler. "That man is dead wrong for having a relationship with a teenager anyway" my dad stated flatly. I explained to him how I had manipulated Tyler. I told him that Allison had told me about how she had done the same thing to my dad. "My goodness what is wrong with you girls?" my dad almost shouted. He was speaking loudly. "You girls are beautiful, smart, and have your whole lives in front of you" he continued. "I was so hurt by how Allison played me" he said softly. "I thought I was going to lose my life over that situation" he stated sadly. "Tyler may not be as understanding as I am, so be careful with his feelings baby" he continued. I wondered how I could have been so stupid to think my dad was like that. I just wanted everything to go back to normal, back to how it was before Allison boned my dad. That's the fantasy I imagined, but there never is any going back. We must live with the results we create within our lives.

I was so busy preparing for my graduation that I didn't notice that Tyler hadn't been to see me or even text me for almost three days. He popped up at my job smiling and jovial. I was glad to see his face. I smiled back at him and waved. "Hi Monay. How are you doing today?"

he asked lightly. "I'm great. How about you?" I replied cheerfully. My mood was great all things considered. I was about to be done with high school finally, and I was getting along great with my dad and my little brother. I was even anxious to clear the air between Tyler and I. We made small talk and planned to meet up later that day. An air of calmness and serenity carried me through the day. I was optimistic about all my dilemmas, and I just knew everything was going to work out beautifully. After I got off work, I went home to change clothes and check the mail. We were still receiving RSVPs from the procrastinators. JJ was making jokes calling me an old maid now that I was graduating. I laughed along with him as I prepared to go meet up with Tyler. I remember thinking that that day was one of the best days I had had in quite a while.

I went over Tyler's house to meet up with him and discuss everything that had been on my mind. When I got there, he hugged me tightly and told me he missed me. I told him the same and let him know that I had a lot on my mind that I had to tell him, he stopped me and started kissing me hungrily. He removed our clothing and fucked me right there in the living room for almost half an hour. Afterward he asked me if I was hungry and I mumbled yes sleepily. He went and got us some Chinese take-out. He had to wake me when he got back home. I looked at him and wondered if I was making a mistake. This man loved me; he could take good care of me as well. Tyler was good looking and could put it down in the bedroom. Second thoughts were clouding my mind heavy right now. On one hand I wanted to break it off with him because of our age difference and the fact that he had a crazy streak hidden barely beneath the surface of his personality. On the other hand, I enjoyed being around him. Tyler was funny, handsome, well spoken, and intelligent. And the sex was out of this world. I don't mean to keep harping on the sex but if you understand then you understand and if you don't, I truly feel for you. Hopefully someday you will get it right and feel exactly how I felt with Tyler. What do I do??

We sat at the kitchen table to eat and talk. "What's on your mind baby?" he asked subtlety. I blurted out everything on my mind except for his craziness. I left that out because it didn't feel right to bring up anything negative at this point in time. He sat there and let me speak for about 20 minutes listening intently. I apologized for manipulating him and asked for his forgiveness. He grabbed both of my hands and looked into my eyes. "Monay I was very upset with you in the beginning" he started. "I wondered why God would allow my life to come crashing down on me like this" he continued. "I thought you were going to ruin my life with some crazy sex scandal shit like we see on TV" he said seriously. "But now I love you Monay. You are the best thing to ever happen to me" he continued. "I will do anything to keep you in my life baby, anything" he stated flatly. "I will not allow anything or anyone to come between us my love" he said. As I listened to him I was swept up with his sincerity. He really did care for me. How could I ever fear the love of my life? Right then and there I decided that I wasn't breaking anything off with Tyler. He was my man and we were going to make a life together. I would tell my dad after my graduation that I was in love and that Tyler and I were going to get married. We made love for the rest of the evening before I went home blissfully exhausted.

The days leading up to graduation were a blur and when it was finally over I felt a sense of relief. After we had dinner I talked to my dad about my future. I decided to attend college right here in Cincinnati at UC. I also discussed me moving out on my own and I could tell that my dad was uncomfortable with that idea. "If you are staying here to attend school why move out?" he asked. He had gotten so upset before about Tyler and me that I wasn't going to bring it up now. I just told him I wanted to be more independent and have my own space. I knew that he was going to discover what was going on but why rock the boat now? Many of my family members had come to wish me well and have dinner for my graduation. It was a great day overall there was only one person on my mind though and that was Tyler. I wanted to hurry up and finish this get together as soon as possible without being obvious about it. When the festivities were finally over, I couldn't wait to see Tyler. He said he had a gift for me and I loved receiving gifts. I busied myself with good byes and thank yous to my family members that came to wish me well on my journey into adulthood. I hoped that I wasn't being rude as I rushed about, but I had places to go and my man to see.

I was so relieved when I finally escaped the hustle and bustle of the graduation festivities. I wanted to see Tyler and discuss our future together. I was so excited that we were really going to be a couple. I thought back to just a couple weeks ago when I was ready to break it off with Tyler. What a mistake that would have been. This man is the love of my life. No young guy could match what Tyler brought to the table. He was handsome, hard-working, and had his money and life together. When I pulled up to his, excuse me, our house I saw Tyler sitting on the porch. I parked and headed to the porch to join him. However, he met me on the sidewalk and hugged me. "Congrats baby" he chimed. Come inside I have something to show you. He took me into the house to show me that he had emptied it out. I mean literally empty. No curtains, no furniture, nothing. I just stared at it in awe. Finally, I asked "Are we moving babe?". "No, we aren't moving love. This is empty because I want you to fill our home with you. You pick out everything baby. The paint colors, the furnishings, the curtains, everything." he stated calmly. I was speechless like wow. This was going to be fun although I had zero experience interior decorating a home. It felt good that Tyler had thought enough of me to have me decorate our home. I hoped that I wouldn't disappoint him.

The next several weeks were a blur because I was moving and decorating and getting accustomed to life as an adult. Allison was recovering and finally walking on her own again. Tyler was like a dream come true. Every day he would make me wonder where this man had been all my life. My life has only been 18 years, but you catch what I mean. He was incredible to put it simply, but he was that plus 50 trillion times incredible. I honestly wondered how I could have ever tried to picture life without Tyler. I'm so grateful that things turned out the way they did. My dad didn't like this situation at all, but he tolerated it because he could tell how happy I was. I honestly wanted for nothing. I wondered where Tyler got so much money, so I asked him about it one day. He explained how his mother and step dad had passed away not long after he and I had started getting serious. The life insurance policies from both parents was substantial he told me. I expressed my condolences, but he hushed me with a wave and a smile.

"Everything happens for a reason baby" he assured me. "You seducing me the way you did was the best thing to ever happen to me Monay" he said seriously looking me directly in my eyes. I Just smiled and told him the same thing. And I really meant it.

One day as I tinkered around in our yard a young man approached me from the sidewalk. "Excuse me miss do you live here?" he asked politely. "Yes sir I do" I replied suspiciously. "I'm sorry to bother you but a good friend of mine used to live here" he said. "I haven't seen him in months his name is Tyler" he continued. "Oh well Tyler still lives here honey. He's my husband." I replied smiling at him. "Oh wow. Husband you say?" he asked surprised. I could tell that he was surprised because of our obvious age difference. "What's your name I will go in the house and tell him he has company?" I asked him. Before he could respond Tyler appeared on the lawn behind me. "Hi love I was just about to come get you. A friend of yours is here" I said quickly. Tyler looked very upset at this person showing up unannounced I suppose that was why he was so angry. I walked away towards the house but stopped at the corner once I was out of sight because I wanted to eaves drop on this conversation. Tyler was the first to speak and he sounded like he was spitting venom. "Why are you here Tony? I told you to never come here again" he hissed at Tony. "So I gather that you're not happy to see me Tyler. Are you happy with your little young bitch?" Tony hissed right back. I was shocked at their interaction. This sounded like a lover's spat. I couldn't stand to hear another word, so I went to our bedroom and sat on the bed dumbfounded.

After several minutes Tyler came back in the house and asked me if I was ok. "Yes I'm fine honey. Are you ok?" I asked him. He just looked at me and shook his head yes. "I have to step out for a bit love. Do you need me to get you anything while I'm out?" he asked. "No thank you" I replied shortly. He left me there alone with my head spinning wondering about my future all of a sudden. I had never met anyone from Tyler's life beside that decrepit bastard Tyrone that helped him do the water heater. The first person I do meet seems to be his estranged lover. Let me slow the fuck down. Maybe it was nothing like I thought. Maybe I was jumping to the wrong conclusion like I did before. My baby will explain this shit tomorrow. I'm going to take a long, hot, bath and meditate on this situation. I had to ask myself what my options were. Ok so let's hypothesize that my man has been sleeping with another man. "What you gonna do bitch?" I asked myself. I would never have even imagined a scenario like this with Tyler. A secret wife or children were things I half expected from a forty-year-old good-looking man. Not this conundrum. How the hell do I compete with a man? I poured myself a large cup of wine and tried to relax.

I awoke the next day refreshed and optimistic about Tyler and me. I could smell bacon and coffee and I was suddenly starving. After brushing my teeth and washing my face I went to the kitchen to address Tyler. He was cooking when I entered the kitchen. "Good morning love" he said cheerfully. "Good morning. Are we going to talk about yesterday? Your friend?" I replied shortly. I needed answers and I wasn't going to slow walk it. "There's really nothing to discuss baby" he replied. "That was not a friend" he continued. "Well what the fuck is he Tyler?" I shouted losing my cool. "He sounded like he was your ex bitch or something" I continued. Tyler made me a plate and approached me calmly. He sat the plate in front of me and grabbed my hands while looking me in my eyes. "I will not allow anything, or anyone to come between us my love" he said solemnly. "That shit yesterday was an unfortunate incident that will never happen again" he continued. I was taken aback by his calmness and sincerity and lost all vestiges of anger. "Please don't hurt me Tyler" I said through tears. "I'm afraid to lose you baby I love you so much it would kill me to lose your love" I whimpered. "Monay you are the best thing to ever happen to me. You are my first and only love" he said to me slowly. After breakfast we made love and fell asleep in each other's arms.

I woke from my nap feeling incredible. Tyler was gone, and I was surprised because I didn't even feel him leave our bed. I thought back to our conversation earlier when he said that I was his first and only love. That sounded too incredible to believe even though it sounded good. I turned on the TV to see if anything interesting was on. Nothing but the news so I left it on and headed to the bathroom. I was stopped in my tracks by the picture on the screen. It was that Tony guy on the news he had been found dead. I was numb as I listened to the story. His body had been dumped in the Ohio river and had washed ashore. Was I dreaming? A cold chill traveled through my body as I sat on the edge of our bed. Was this Tyler's way of keeping anyone or anything from interfering with our relationship? I was opened up to that uncertainty again. "Am I losing my fucking mind" I asked myself. Just because that dude is dead doesn't mean Tyler had anything to do with it. I had to stop jumping to these crazy assumptions because I was driving myself nuts. I resolved to stop postulating and find out once and for all what was going on with my mystery lover. I bought myself a few GPS tracker devices to put on and around Tyler, so I could monitor his movements. I had to know what he was doing when we weren't together.

For the most part Tyler's movements were repetitive. His every day activities didn't vary at all. The only place he went that I wasn't familiar with was a home in Forest Park which was on the other side of town. I researched the address and it came back to Tyler being the owner. He visited this house 2 to 3 times per week without fail. When I drove past it the grass was cut and the home looked well-kept and lived in. I watched the house for hours at a time looking for any signs of life, but the only life at this house was when Tyler came over to keep up the place. Maybe it was his parent's old home. Maybe it was just a rental property that isn't rented at the moment. As I watched the mystery house Tyler pulled into the driveway and opened the garage door. There was a dark colored SUV in there. I couldn't distinguish the color from this distance. That vehicle flashed across my memory because a dark colored SUV hit Allison. A shiver traveled slowly up my spine as I contemplated Tyler being a murdering sociopathic homosexual. This was too much to take, so I drove away sad but determined. I needed to talk with someone I could trust no matter what. I needed advice that wasn't tainted by some hidden agenda. I needed my dad.

My dad and I sat in the living room as I told him everything that had happened as well as everything I was thinking. He listened closely without responding until I was done. "Wow I'm not even gonna say I told you so" he started. He looked me in my eyes sadly with tears in his eyes. "You and Allison just never know what you are getting yourselves into" he said quietly. "Manipulating men in this way is just wrong baby. You guys think it's cute huh? Get you a sugar daddy huh? Well now what? Allison almost died? Your scared now? You should have been scared before all of this mess got started" he finished flatly. I could tell that my dad was disappointed in me and that hurt. "I know a private investigator who can check Tyler out for us" he said. "You should move back home immediately Monay" he stated. "No dad not yet. I don't want to make him suspicious" I replied. He just shook his head and walked away. I felt a lot better now that I had my dad on my team. I figured that it was a win win situation because if there was no evidence of foul play then I would be able to trust Tyler again. If it comes out that Tyler is a very sick puppy, I can leave him without any drama. The plan was perfect what could possibly go wrong?

Almost 3 weeks went by without any word from the P.I. and I was starting to get antsy. Tyler had been great so there were no complaints there, but in the back of my mind I needed answers to feel secure about our relationship. My dad called me and asked me to meet him at Olive Garden for a bite. He knows I love the chicken alfredo there. When I arrived my dad and the P.I. were already sitting together talking intently. They both stood up when I got to the table. "Hi, I'm Phillip Hall private investigator" said the P.I. extending his hand for a shake. I shook his hand and told him my name then we all sat down. "Your friend Tyler has been through a lot" he told me. He then proceeded to describe everything he had discovered. Tyler was born in Michigan. His dad died when he was very young like 5 or 6 years old. His mom met his step dad a year or so later and they got married. They never had any more children. It was suspected in Michigan that the step dad was sexually abusing Tyler, but no charges were ever filed, and they moved to Cincinnati in the midst of that ordeal. Nothing interesting happened all these years until he met you Monay. It seems that right after he met you both of his parents died suddenly. There wasn't any investigation into it because it seemed like an accident by elderly people. But it does seem suspicious now because of everything else that has been happening. They both died in the garage from carbon monoxide poisoning. The authorities suspected that they had been warming up the car without raising the door and subsequently died.

Mr. Hall was very thorough in his investigation. He described the Tony guy as Tyler's suspected lover. "I can't say with absolute certainty that they were lovers, but I can tell you that there is no indication that Tyler has been with any female before you Monay" he stated. "There are no old pictures, no proms, no dates, nothing at all. It's quite strange actually" he continued. Tyler did say that I was his first and only love. Now I was thinking that he really meant what he said. Mr. Hall continued "I believe that SUV in his garage was used to run over your friend Allison". "I believe Tyler killed Tony and his parents because of you Monay" he continued. "I think that any person who gets in between you and Tyler will be in grave danger" he warned. "That applies to you as well my dear. Tread carefully with this guy" he continued. I was wondering how I could possibly get away from this nut. "I have alerted the police about my suspicions and they are going to check out that SUV" stated Mr. Hall. "In the mean time I would advise extreme caution when dealing with Tyler" he warned us. My dad was shaking his head with his eyes closed. I could tell he was wondering how I could have possibly picked this guy of all guys.

This nightmare was like a gift from Satan that just keeps giving. I truly loved Tyler. Still do actually. I kind of feel sorry for him. What if he was raised thinking that the relationship between him and his step dad was normal. What if he never had an opportunity to be with a female and when he finally does get with a female, he realizes what he has been missing out on, so he kills his mom and step-dad. He would obviously blame them for keeping him blind to how good some young pussy like mine is. This pussy has caused this man to murder 3 people and harm a 4th person. Wow so this is my fault. If I would have never given Tyler this pussy those people would still be living. I don't like the idea of having killer pussy. I thought I had it all figured out. I thought I knew what I was doing. I was so wrong. I was so stupid. "Please forgive me Lord" I said to myself. I had to figure out how I was going to stay away from Tyler. I was shook just thinking about what he was obviously capable of. Killing someone was nothing to him. His heart was cold.

My mind wandered all over the place as I thought about all that had happened. I will stay in Dayton over one of my girl's house until the police arrest Tyler. "Great idea Monay" I told myself as I got on the interstate headed to Dayton.

I didn't want to endanger Allison any further, so I avoided her like the plague. I figured that Tyler didn't know about Camryn, so I went to her house to shack up a few days. She was cool with it. I left out most of the reason why I wanted to stay with her because I didn't want to alarm her. The less she knew I reasoned the better off she would be. We played around and reminisced about our adventures as kids. I could tell she wanted to ease my mind, and she did somewhat. My mind and heart just kept going back to Tyler and the horrible predicament I had created being a hot in the ass little girl. My selfishness had cost lives and harm to others and I would never forgive myself. Destiny came over also and we all laughed and giggled like little girls enjoying life. For a small moment my mind cleared of the drama I was going through. I had great friends and I really appreciated what they were doing without either of them really knowing what they were doing for me. A couple days passed without any word from my dad or about Tyler. I was beginning to think that maybe he had skipped town. On the third day my dad called me hysterical. "Is JJ with you Monay?" he asked nervously. "No dad I have been in Dayton hiding out. I haven't even talked to JJ since I left" I replied getting nervous myself. "He hasn't come home from school baby and I'm really worried" he gasped. "I'm on my way dad" I assured him. I thanked my friends and hit the highway headed home mind racing.

I arrived at my dad's house worried about my little brother because he was a good kid. He never did anything out of the ordinary like not coming straight home from school. My dad opened the door with tears in his eyes. "I'm calling the cops Monay something is wrong. My boy would never have his father worrying like this" he cried. I have never seen my father shook like this, seeing him like this was making me worry more. The phone ringing interrupted the hysteria for the moment. I answered the phone and my blood turned cold as I heard the voice on the other end of the phone. "Hello Monay baby" Tyler said calmly. "Where have you been hiding baby?" he continued. My dad saw my reaction and was shouting "who is it?" repeatedly. I couldn't speak for a few moments. When I caught my breath and regained my voice I tried to speak calmly into the phone. "Hi Tyler. Right now isn't a good time to talk. We have a family emergency going on" I told him as calmly as I could. "I know all about your family emergency Monay. I'm calling because I watched you as you entered your dad's house. Your little brother is right here with me" he said coldly. "If you ever want to see this little bastard again you need to come see about me" he continued. "I'm on my way baby" I stuttered. I hung up the phone and turned to face my dad. "Tyler has JJ dad" I said quietly.

My father was enraged and quietly began to plan Tyler's demise. "I'm going to go talk to him dad" I said forcefully. "No you're not" my dad countered. "Then that fucking maniac will have both of my babies" he continued. "Dad I have to do this. This is all my fault and I must fix this" I responded looking him in the eyes. I grabbed my dad's hands and assured him that I would bring back JJ. I was equally perturbed though I had to be calm for my dad too. My dad agreed hesitantly. My dad has raised us around guns and ammo and how to use them properly, so when I started to understand my situation more, I began to arm myself and any areas that we could possibly find ourselves. All in all, I had four guns hidden in different places around our house. I really loved Tyler, but I was also very frightened of him. How can I love someone and be afraid of them at the same time? Something must really be wrong with me I thought to myself. My fear was over powered by my love for my little brother. He was innocent in all this, and now he's another victim of my stupidity.

When I arrived at our house…I mean Tyler's house I parked where I always park. I acted like I always act. I looked around the yard observing where work was required. I had to attempt normalcy because I was amped up and wired. Tyler joined me outside in the yard before I could even make it to the door. He looked so handsome I was taken aback, I just stared at his face for several seconds. "Where's JJ?" I asked him quietly. "Hey baby" he responded totally ignoring my question. "Hey baby" I countered looking him in the eye. This entire situation was making my stuff extra moist. For a moment I rationalized on how inappropriate these thoughts and feelings were in this space in time, but that shit floated away on the air like fart fumes. I could clearly look in this man's face and know without any doubt that he loved me unconditionally. I knew that he would do nothing to hurt me. We hugged and looked at each other for an awkward moment that felt perfect. At that moment I would die for this man. He just needed to send JJ back to my dad so we could do us.

We hugged for a long moment before he started to speak. "Monay I'm so sorry for this. I just didn't know what to do. You have been avoiding me. I haven't hurt your brother he's in the house playing video games" Tyler said sadly. "Don't move let me see your hands" yelled a police officer. I was shocked. Tyler just stared at my face with a smirk on his lips. Everything happened so suddenly but at the same time it was like slow motion. To this day I can describe in great detail the events of that day. I relive those moments every day some days repeatedly. Tyler grabbed me around my neck with his left arm and pulled out a gun with his right hand. He started shooting at the police officers wounding several of them in the process. My dad and JJ were both critically injured. Thank God they both survived. I didn't find out about my dad and brother until after they were being put in the ambulance. I cried so hard not knowing if my dad and brother were ok. How could I have been so stupid? After I had calmed down and the cops were finished questioning me for the moment, I made my way to the hospital. Thank God they were both going to be ok.

I lived at the hospital as my dad and my little brother recovered. I felt so guilty about everything that had happened. My family is forever scarred by this entire situation. Some simple-minded asshole asked to write a book about our predicament, and we kicked his ass. Me and my cousins were chilling outside our people's house smoking and chopping it up. Here comes this dimwit talking book and movie deals. Maybe we were all traumatized or mad or just not in the mood for dumb shit. Whatever the reason we beat that fool down. Even after that drama the days were filled with thrill seekers, news reporters, and nosy motherfuckers all up in your business. I struggled between my love for my dad and my brother, and my feelings for Tyler. I still have a profound feeling of affection for that man. I truly felt like a piece of shit because I knew my dad and brother could never forgive Tyler. I still loved Tyler though. What was a girl to do? Tyler left me some nice finances to oversee, plus a couple homes. He left me in charge of all of his business interests. This life was crazy.

As the next several weeks played out, I was sickened by the characterizations given to Tyler by the prosecutors and media sources covering our dilemma. He was portrayed as a sick pedophile murderer. They were so wrong. If only they knew him the way I did. Tyler was convicted of attempted murder, kidnapping, and child endangerment. He was sentenced to 15 years to life and I wanted to die. What would I do? What should I do? My dad couldn't know about any of the business. Since I was 18, I didn't require my dad's consent. He absolutely despised Tyler to the point that he wanted that man dead. But all glory to God that my dad and my brother survived without any major complications. We all rehabbed together. I wasn't hurt but I went through it all with my loved ones regardless. Everything bad that happened could be directly attributed to me with a very high accuracy percentage. I attempted to rationalize it all. I tried to bring sense to it all, but there was no rationality there was no sense to this tragedy. Follow your first mind or at least your second mind is the best advice I can share with all of you.

Our lives proceeded without any incidents. Calm was the storm that had been our lives for a long time. Too long have we tiptoed around the elephant. The elephant was my immature sexual nature and selfishness. I was just as guilty as I held my tongue. In my mind I just wanted all of the attention on me and Tyler to go away. I was so tired of people commenting about how strong I was. About my outstanding qualities. "Shut the fuck up!" I wanted to shout. They just didn't know that my dilemma was self-inflicted. Only silence as I daydreamed about what I should say, and about what I should do. I did nothing but think about all of that. A very fleeting, a very soft thought crossed my mind about what I was doing. Was I still being a stupid hot in the ass little bitch? "Oh well" I said out loud to myself. My finances were in good shape thanks to Tyler. I continued my education making moves to become an attorney. With everything that has occurred over the last several years I still find myself trying to give logic and rationality to emotions. Sometimes "it is what it is" my uncle used to tell me.

Through it all I still felt a very strong desire for Tyler. Thoughts of him consumed my days and nights. I was so sprung. I attempted to hook up with guys but it never could work out because I still belonged to Tyler. I could never share my feelings with my dad or anyone else. I kept my feelings for Tyler close to my heart. No one could ever know about my true feelings. As long as Tyler knows no one else matters. I will wait for my love. I write him letters under an assumed name that can't be traced to me. Love is a trip sometimes...

Printed in the United States
By Bookmasters